Soft Answers to Hard Feelings

by
Darl Andersen

Copyright, 1998
5th Printing - April. 1998

Darl Andersen
648 North Orange
Mesa, Arizona
(602) 833-3200

Distributed by
Granite Publishing
Orem, Utah

Contents

1	Love Your Minister Neighbor	1
2	To Have Clergy Friends, Be One	3
3	How to Start Clergy Communications	6
4	Unkind Feelings	9
5	How Can We Share So They Enjoy It?	12
6	What Do Mormons Have That We Don't?	14
7	Rev. Jim, Why Do You Feel Unkind Toward LDS?	17
8	Is the Millennium Near?	20
9	The Golden Rule in Action	23
10	LDS Sermons From a Protestant Pulpit?	26
11	On Whose Side Am I?	29
12	Minister's Children Join LDS Church	33
13	Parallel Positions to Protestant Points	36
14	Impossible to Know How He Did It?	39
15	How Did the Book of Mormon get Printed?	42
16	How Can I Believe the Book of Mormon?	45
17	Similarities between the Apostle Paul and Joseph Smith	48
18	Living Prophets	52
19	A Prophet, Key to Sacrifice	55
20	Who Is of the Apostasy?	58
21	Who Has the Lord's Gifts?	61
22	Temple Wedding - Parents Excluded	63
23	The Endowment - A Gift of Understanding	66
24	Do Mormons Believe In a Physical God?	70

25	Mormons Become Gods?	73
26	Do Missionaries Steal Sheep?	76
27	Are Mormons Devious Friends?	79
28	Church of Christ or Cult of Satan?	81
29	Hypocrisy - The Dreaded Disease of Religious Leaders	85
30	Christ-Centered or Self-Centered?	88
31	A Burden on My Shoulders	91
32	The Golden Rule	94

FORWARD

This little book began by accident in Palmyra, New York where my wife Erma and I were serving a senior couple mission as host guides at the Grandin Building, where the Book of Mormon was first printed.

As missionaries from all over the world came to tour the Grandin Building, I would occasionally relate stories of some of the discussions and experiences I had had with ministers about Mormonism.

Missionaries persuaded me to put some of these stories on paper to help them in their discussions. The stories were often reduced in length to fit on one page for easy copying and distribution. There was no thought of them being in a book.

Later, as we prepared for another mission to Seattle Washington, Erma suggested that these stories should be bound into a unit to be preserved for our many grandchildren when they would serve as missionaries.

Since then, requests for copies have required additional printings of many thousands of copies.

Some changes in this sixth printing have been made to provide increased clarity of the ideas and concepts contained in these stories to help those committed to serving the Lord and their neighbors.

I have also added a story or two that I have felt impressed would make it more usable to all. I have felt that more good can be achieved by remembering that in the great religions in the world, the Golden Rule is an underlying tenant. If we simply remember to "treat others the way we would like them to treat us", we will find much greater satisfaction in our service to our fellow men.

As the years go by, I also find "new" discoveries that I feel need to be explored and discussed. It is jolting to ponder how much we don't know, *and don't know that we don't know it!* It seems that with the wisdom that comes with age, we realize others know so much we don't, and compared to our creator, we are all simple dummies.

Human tendencies of pride and ill will close our eyes to these facts, so we judge and condemn others, ignoring their knowledge and virtues. When I abuse my neighbor's inspiring faith, I act like a "fool and blind hypocrite" as explained by the all-wise creator I profess to follow.

Joy is felt in respect and supporting goodness of others. Misery comes with disrespect and opposition. We are both happy and smart when we follow the Golden Rule.

I express my gratitude to many who have pushed, prodded and assisted, to enable me to bring this project to completion. My sweet wife Erma did so much in editing and proofreading. Many suggestions came from a good friend, Bruce Cox, to whom I am eternally grateful. His vision and comprehension of these principles are thrilling.

Darl Andersen

Preface

Try to imagine what five hundred different clergymen would tell you about Mormonism if you asked them as a friend. Latter-day Saints would be astounded to look at themselves through minister eyes. They would see how their actions often cause ill will instead of goodwill. This is a tragedy.

Since ministers are public opinion makers about the LDS faith, any feelings of ill will severely effect public opinion about the LDS Church and it's doctrines.

Both LDS and non-LDS religious leaders are motivated by integrity to share with others the message each feels is divinely sent to bless the lives of those who will receive it. That common goal is worthy and acceptable. But negative feelings are caused in the process when there is not enough respect, support for common values and understanding shown to each other.

Try to comprehend the tremendous benefits for goodwill and understanding if LDS could clearly see what they do that causes ill will and opposition. Then they could make simple changes to show respect and provide soft answers to those who feel offended.

This tragedy cries out for LDS action because only Latter-day Saints can provide the respect that will bring goodwill and give the soft answers that will bring understanding. How can this be done?

In his twenty-five years of practicing his hobby of taking ministers to lunch Brother Andersen has provided clear evidence that this tragedy can be easily avoided by following the way the Savior taught. *First* He gave service that built bridges to people; *Then*, with love and compassion he offered answers to bring relief from life's burdens. *When people were interested,* He taught them his doctrine (for the salvation of their eternal lives). The use of these steps is so vividly demonstrated in the Book of Mormon story of Ammon and King Lamoni. (Please read Alma 17:21-39).

May you enjoy this exciting experience as much as we the publishers have.

CHAPTER 1

Love Your Minister Neighbor

An exciting opportunity to extend the blessings of the Gospel of Jesus Christ to many more of God's children will come from being friends to our religious neighbors! The Lord has told us how—just live the great commandment "Love thy neighbor as thyself".

Ministers are the main source of public opinion about the LDS Church, and they are our neighbors in a very special way who need our love and service. Their vocation is to teach of the Lord and help those in need.

But most ministers find little effort from LDS to suggest a desire to be friends or share understanding with them. It is simply unrealistic to expect these ministers to make positive and correct statements about the LDS Church when they do not understand, nor have friends among their LDS neighbors.

The natural result is that a great deal of false information and ill will is spread about the LDS faith. The Gospel of Christ, as believed by Latter-day Saints is a message of love, beauty, and inspiration. Only those who look for that beauty through friendly eyes can possibly understand it.

Latter-day Saints are the only ones who can correct this unacceptable situation. Surely the Lord expects His servants to melt away this stumbling block in the pathway of His Kingdom of love. The Church of Jesus Christ of Latter-day Saints was established to be *a light unto the world*, to help show people the way to *come unto Christ.*

To have a friend is to be one.

To receive respect and goodwill is to give it.

If we can be friends to these men and women who try to be honest and professional in serving the Lord, then they will be our friends, and will help build a spirit in our communities that will promote the Kingdom of God.

If every minister could have a faithful Latter-day Saint friend to enjoy, and effectively communicate with, the whole image and impact of the Church would soon improve, for ministers are the source and vehicle that spreads religious reactions that vitally effect the image and impact of the Church.

Most ministers are quite mature and charitable. If they are convinced of our sincerity, they will accept our "biased" points of view, as they do their own. As we share understanding with genuine feelings of love, the Holy Spirit can and will work miracles.

The stories in this book are written in the hope that they will help us honestly communicate goodwill and friendship to religious leaders. The good people of all faiths must know we are their friends and allies in the work of helping people to know God and live close to Him. We share with them the common purposes to stem the tide of sin and evil, and give service to those in need. We really need each other.

❖

CHAPTER 2

To Have Clergy Friends, Be One

Palmyra, New York is known for the four Protestant churches located on one cross street intersection. Part of our missionary assignment there was to help the people of the churches in Palmyra gain a better understanding and good will toward members of the Church of Jesus Christ of Latter-day Saints. As my wife and I prayerfully approached this unusual challenge, and tried to find ways to accomplish our task, some simple truths began to stand out and give us answers:

1. A friend will look for the good in you and amplify it, while an opponent will look for the bad and amplify that.
2. To have a friend is to be one. Usually our religious neighbors don't view LDS as friends. So the first step was to be their friends and amplify the good in them.
3. A Christian is commanded to 'Love his neighbor as himself'. If we profess and don't do it — "say and do not" — we gain no favor before the Lord, or our religious neighbors.

4. The people of other churches are definitely our neighbors. We have to love them in the same way we want them to love us — like the Golden Rule admonishes.
5. Ministers are the main source of public opinion and attitude about the LDS Church. So it seemed urgent to assist and communicate with these leaders.
6. Ministers' basic goals are to persuade people to believe in Jesus Christ and follow Him. These goals are so much like our own, and worthy of our eager support.
7. Most religious leaders want to be professional in their positions of service to people. It is difficult to be professional in our callings if we do not know and appreciate the benefits that our neighbor finds in his faith.
8. Religious leaders are committed to serve the Lord and their neighbors. But we do not serve the Lord nor our neighbor when we say untrue or unkind things about our neighbor's faith.
9. To gain understanding and good will is rarely a one way street. As we give, so shall we receive. If we want it, we have to give it.
10. When we share our faith and testimonies with religious leaders the benefits may be multiplied many times when they share with those they serve.

Considering these facts, we went to the ministers in Palmyra with the specific purposes to:
1. Encourage them in their individual commitment to bring people to believe in Jesus Christ and keep His commandments;
2. Build their image in the community as leaders who lift standards of behavior in the town, schools and service clubs to find a better life;

3. Eagerly serve with them in worthy projects such as family week; and
4. Share information on LDS programs that may benefit families, youth, the public, welfare, etc.

Understanding and goodwill were the natural results. When these ministers became convinced that our motives were genuine (to be of service to them, to share understanding and good will — not to proselyte, bash or brag) communication quickly opened up. Our exchange was honest and revealing. Mutual understanding grew at an exciting rate. Our efforts were fruitful and rewarding.

We provided them with what they wanted — respect, goodwill, understanding and support. In return, they gave those same things back to us, and these were the very things we wanted from them.

The Lord prayed to the Father that those who believed on Him might be one so that the world could know of His divine mission. As we live to answer His prayer, we find the answers to our own challenges.

CHAPTER 3

How to Start Clergy Communications

At a monthly missionary report meeting of the Maricopa Stake, the missionary sisters present, with tears in their eyes, told of two separate families who had been just so 'golden' last week, but this week had completely changed from attitudes of receptiveness to those of negative antagonism. What had caused such an abrupt reversal? After considerable discussion, it was suggested that since I knew one of the families I should go to these families and try to find out why.

Each of the families readily explained to me that the change in their attitude had come from talking with their ministers. I could hardly believe what they said the ministers had told them. Not only had these Ministers caused the contacts to feel unkind toward the Mormons, but they were embarrassed to think they had been so gullible as to let the missionaries in at all.

Why would professed servants of God say such ugly and untrue things about another's beautiful faith? These were men we often worked with in Boy Scouts, United Fund, YMCA, City and Schools. Did they really believe such awful things? Did ministers really feel so bitter toward Mormon Christians? Would they give me answers to these questions if I asked them?

In a determined effort to find out, I took three simple questions and went individually to six of the leading clergymen in town. The questions were:
1. What can Mormons do to be better neighbors?
2. What can Mormons do to support your good Christian influence in Mesa?
3. What can we do to open channels of communication to understand each other?

Some of their reactions were so accusing that I was just shocked. One of the ministers was rather cutting with his remarks and I began to respond in kind. But remembering that my purpose was to find out 'why', and not to 'straighten him out', I asked him if we were mature enough men to discuss our problems without acting childish? To amplify I said, "Evidently we have problems that need discussion and solutions. It seems we are neither addressing the problems nor looking for the solutions."

That was a jolt for this forthright man, and he quickly asked what I was driving at, and where could we discuss our problems?

I mentioned that most Christian ministers in Mesa met in a clergy council to discuss their mutual needs and problems. Mormons were excluded with the excuse that "they are not Christian". I suggested that since he knew Mormons were as Christian as his or any other Christian group in town this clergy council might be one place we could talk together.

Immediately he asked if we would come if invited. Since he was then chairman of the clergy association, he would get us invited.

In a couple of weeks he called to say that some of the ministers could not, in good conscience, accept Mormons into the association. But would I come as an 'Observer?'

I was happy to accept this invitation since I could not officially represent the LDS church there anyway. It would be a pleasure to attend as an observer.

The meetings were most enjoyable and informative. They provided an excellent opportunity for considerable pleasant communication. Soon I was invited to serve on some committees.

Looking back, it is so clear that having a sincere willingness to communicate, to be honestly helpful and to try to understand without criticism of my minister neighbors has paid off in precious returns. Some of these men are our family's most cherished friends. Exciting gains have come in building bridges of understanding and good will, and some very significant benefits have come to The Church of Jesus Christ of Latter day Saints. I am certain that the action that was in progress to sever relations between Arizona State University and Brigham Young University over the Black Issue was stopped by the concerned influence of these, my minister friends.

I am also certain that the significant paper distributed nation wide by the National Conference of Christians and Jews, about the "God Makers" film, was made possible by the strong support of these minister friends. It brings a lump to my throat to think of the rich service received from these great people because they felt from us a little genuine love and honest concern for them.

❖

CHAPTER 4

Unkind Feelings

Our son-in-law, Fred, had been raised in a family in which the father was a Protestant minister for twenty-five years, so Fred understood how ministers react to their LDS neighbors. Years later Fred invited me to speak at a Tucson, Arizona Stake High Priest's fireside on the subject of "How LDS offend their religious neighbors".

It frightened me as I wrote down the many things that I knew of that are offensive, especially when LDS are seldom aware of offending and seldom consider changes. Perhaps it would be helpful if LDS could see themselves through ministers' eyes. Then they would be aware of some of these problems that ministers have expressed to me:

1. RESPECT: Mormons seldom show respect or express appreciation to ministers for their tremendous contribution to Christian faith and behavior in our communities.
2. COMMUNICATION: LDS leaders rarely communicate with other church leaders. Any relationship —

family, business, church — without communication usually has trouble.

3. FRIENDS: Mormons don't seem interested in making friends with ministers. Usually any contact is seen as an opportunity to proselyte, brag or bash — not to make friends.
4. PROSELYTIZING: This word is loathsome to many clergymen. To them it is plain 'sheep stealing', not sharing faith and love or giving answers.
5. BRAGGING: With excitement Mormons tell of their successful church programs — youth, welfare, missionary, etc. To those who don't want to hear it, that is plain bragging.
6. BASHING: Mormons eagerly discuss their 'rational theology', well supported by scripture. Defending beliefs of faith often becomes an unpleasant bash.
7. SUPERIORITY: Claims of 'new truth' from Heaven and the 'Fullness of the Gospel' are perceived as an attitude of superiority and 'looking down the nose' at them.
8. NEW SCRIPTURE: Most churches feel their foundation of truth and authority is found in the Bible. To admit 'new scripture' is like breaking up their foundation.
9. DIVINE AUTHORITY: Mormon claims to 'exclusive authority' in the Lord's 'own' church tends to make them feel second class and unacceptable to the Lord in their service.
10. RESTORATION: If Mormons have the Lord's original church restored, what do they have?
11. LIVING PROPHETS: If anyone does not follow living prophets they are in trouble.
12. ATTACKS: When ministers give their heart and soul to serve the Lord the best they know, how can anyone say they don't teach the truth or don't have the Lord's authority?

13. LANGUAGE: Each religion gives unique meanings to words and expressions which limit understanding of each other to some degree.
14. DOCTRINAL CHASMS: LDS are inclined to magnify differences which tend to choke off understanding rather than build bridges from similarities.
15. EXCLUDING: Non-member parents can not view temple weddings of their own LDS family members. This is a festering, ongoing source of resentment.
16. CLICKISHNESS: Much Mormon conversation is about their church since their church touches all dimensions of their lives. Non-members can feel left out and isolated.
17. UNPAID CLERGY: It is irritating when an unpaid Bishop and volunteer staff perform as well as a paid minister and professional staff.
18. COMMITMENT: LDS acceptance of and commitment to a call such as a call to be a bishop or missionary amazes and frustrates other church leaders who would like to see similar commitment among their members.
19. MONEY: Perceived Mormon wealth with churches paid for and many tithe payers is an envy to many who don't have it.
20. LOVE: Ministers hope the gospel proclaimed by LDS — love of neighbor, the golden rule and charity, the true love of Christ — will be more evident in LDS actions toward them.

The list can go on and on when there are unkind feelings and ill will. *What can LDS do? Love them.* Love them and communicate with them. The Lord gave all of us that commandment. It will solve the problems. With a little concern and preparation each of these irritations can be easily softened to promote goodwill and understanding.

❖

CHAPTER 5

How Can We Share So They Enjoy It?

How can we share the precious beauties of our faith with those who have other deep religious convictions? How can we present a differing concept without arousing an attitude of conflict and antagonism that prevents understanding?

The following guidelines have been used effectively to provide open and enjoyable dialogue with many ministers and other church leaders.

1. ATTITUDE - Recognize and lift up the goodness in them.

2. GOALS - Establish common basic goals and purposes such as helping people to: a) Love the Lord and keep the commandments. b) love their neighbors as themselves. c) Find joy in life. d) Live and teach *The Golden Rule*. Most every Christian leader can support these goals.

3. CHURCH - Consider the Church in light of its fruit, or success, in reaching these goals. The Church then is viewed as a means to the end, a tool, a method, or a divine guide to bless lives. Instead of the conflict of one church against another, each

person may honestly and openly appreciate the success and value of the Church in reaching the goal. It is hard for anyone to be negative toward good fruit. The Lord's measure is "by their fruits."

4. DOCTRINE - Explain doctrine and theology as it relates to and produces behavior. Doctrine then has relevance and value with here and now desirable results. For example: The strength and unity of LDS families comes through believing in temple marriage and the eternal family unit. Most honorable men can develop respect, and usually a positive attitude toward the Church.

5. BLESSINGS - Speak in the first person. When talking about the blessing and advantages of the Church, avoid using the third person approach. Such as: "*They* should accept and be blessed." Also avoid speaking in second person. For instance: "*You* should see and believe." Talk in *first* person, "The richness and priceless blessings of the Church to *me* are these. In this way, a desire may be developed in the listener to enjoy what you have.

6. LOVE - The most acceptable motivation to bring change in a person's thought or action is a sincere love and concern for the person involved. Satisfying self ego or ulterior motives bring negative reactions. Even loving and serving the Lord and His Church must find its fulfillment in loving and feeding individuals. As the Master said to Peter, "If you love me, feed my sheep." We may sometimes stumble in our efforts to bless a person, but if he feels we have sincere concerns for him, there is seldom conflict.

I am deeply convinced that with the proper attitude and open communication, unkindness and antagonism toward the Church can be *loved* away. If we really feel we enjoy blessings from the Lord that would bring happiness to others, we must find ways to surmount existing barriers, and freely share so that they, also, may have these blessings from the Lord.

❖

CHAPTER 6

What Do Mormons Have That We Don't?

The man on the phone said he was Father O. from the local Diocese on the Catholic church. Some one had told him that I could help him obtain information about the Family Home Evening program used by the Church of Jesus Christ of Latter-day Saints. I was glad to respond, so I took some of our old Home Evening manuals with me and bought his lunch. During lunch I told him most everything I could about this LDS church program.

Both of us agreed that the Family Home Evening program is an effective and enjoyable way to benefit families. It seemed appropriate for every church to adopt such a method to enhance unity and spiritual strength among its families.

During a searching discussion, Father O. asked me what percentage of Latter-day Saint families actually held a "Family Home Evening" each week. I told him that in the stake in which I lived, the church reports showed nearly 50 percent average participation. He responded with surprise that the figure was so high.

His next questions were: What percent of Mormon young men go on missions for the church? What percent of Latter-day Saint marriages are in the temple? What percent of church members pay tithing? What percent attend church services each Sunday?

I replied that to the best of my information, the answers to these questions were all about 50 percent in our Stake. Some more and some less. Over and over again, Father O. expressed surprise that these percentages were so high. He wondered how such a large number of LDS church members could be persuaded to participate, and often to sacrifice for church programs and activities.

Thoughtfully, Father O. then asked this penetrating question. "What do you have in the Mormon Church that we do not have in the Catholic Church to cause such remarkable commitment?" Finding a way to give an accurate answer to that question in a way he would understand and relate to, was a real challenge for me. After a fast prayer, the answer came out something like this:

"Probably what the Mormons have that causes such a noticeable response is what they call a "personal testimony" that Jesus Christ really lives and loves us; that He has a church - His church - here on earth which He personally directs through a living prophet. Mormons believe this prophet then communicates to the members of the Church specific callings and programs "from the Lord" for them to follow.

"Mormon Christians believe that the Church of Jesus Christ of Latter-day Saints was organized as a result of the actual appearance of God the Father and His Son Jesus Christ to a prophet. They believe that more specific instructions came with appearances of Peter, James and John, and others who had lived anciently, who conveyed to men the specific authority to act for the Lord. The impact and power of such beliefs produces commitment in believers quite similar to that demonstrated by the early Saints at the time of Christ, who also had similar beliefs.

"Although these beliefs may be offensive to those who do not share them, still such "personal testimonies" are the basic reason for the noticeable commitment of those who believe. If I, as a typical member of the church, really believe that the Lord lives and loves me, that He has His church which He personally directs through a living prophet, and that prophet has called on me to hold a weekly Family Home Evening, or go on a mission, or pay tithing, or be active in the church, probably I will do it – even if it means some sacrifice."

The clear thinking and perceptive judgement of Father O. came through when he said, "It looks like about 50 percent of you Mormons really believe".

A sobering observation, but how fortunate those fifty percent are to have a personal testimony.

The Phoenix Diocese introduced a Family Night program which was evidently quite successful for several years. It was an honor for me to be a part of helping to strengthen families around us. How can we more effectively share with each other successful church programs?

CHAPTER 7

"Rev. Jim, Why Do You Feel Unkind Toward LDS?"

"Reverend Jim, do you know why you have unkind feelings toward me because I am Mormon? Can you tell me why, so I can understand?" I asked.

Rev. Jim was our friend visiting in our home. He tried to answer the question honestly. After some thought, he gave this explanation:

"It seems that through all Jewish history, the Jews have been persecuted. Why? Probably because they claim to be a chosen people of God, with a special lineage and a divine mission. As a result, they appear to think they are superior, and favored of God.

"Now you know that nobody can stand somebody who thinks he is superior. So the Jews have been a persecuted people. This persecution has been the natural and human response to their claims of being superior.

"Now, it is the same way with you Mormons. You go around saying you have God's exclusive authority—that only through your Priesthood are God's special blessings available. You claim you have the pipeline to God—that He speaks His will through your prophets. You think you are superior to the rest of us.

"It isn't your doctrine that bothers me. Doctrine is just an excuse. I really don't care about your kooky doctrine—maybe mine is kooky, too—but I just can't stand it when you act superior and look down your nose at me. To be very honest, it makes me feel unkind toward you and inclined to fight you back."

When my response was that I didn't feel superior or look down my nose at him, he said, "Yes, you do, and don't argue with me."

So to find a "parallel" that might help him understand my feelings, I said, "Well, OK, suppose I do. But what about you? Do you think you are superior and look down your nose at those who are not Christians? Do you believe you have God's authority, and that only through Jesus Christ can a person come to God?—do you accept Christ's statement when he said, "I am the way, the truth and the life, and no man cometh to the Father but by me?" Do you feel Christians have the pipeline to God in that through the New Testament and the Christian Church, God's will is made known?

"Is your attitude toward the non-Christian nearly identical to what you say the LDS attitude is toward you? Surely you believe you have something from a divine source to share with those who do not believe as you do—that you have some additional truths from heaven, which are not just philosophies of men."

He answered that he had never thought of it that way before.

It seems that this has been the situation throughout religious history. Whenever anyone claimed to have received authority or truth from God, they were accused of feeling superior and looking down their noses toward those without.

So the very human response to "fight back" helps explain why prophets of God have been persecuted and stoned throughout much of Biblical history. Probably this is a big reason why the Savior himself was put to death. It was no doubt the reason that Jesus could prophesy that His followers would be persecuted.

Religious strife and contention are nearly always the result of injured pride. When some make claims of superior authority and truth from God, the human response is to fight back. So ill will and unkind feelings spread even among those who preach love and goodwill.

Can we hope for the time when the "Spirit of the Lord" will be felt enough to temper the "lusts of the flesh" and prevent unkind feelings and negative reactions?

Can we, as some of the most professing preachers of the golden Rule, practice what we preach? Can we do for others what we want them to do for us so that they will do it for us? Though that is not always easy to do, it is surely the "Way to Happiness," and the way to obtain the desired results.

CHAPTER 8

Is the Millenium Near?

In the Mesa newspaper, a small article stated that in Tempe, Arizona, the Faculty Senate of Arizona State University was scheduled to vote soon on a proposed action to sever inter-scholastic relations with Brigham Young University because of the Mormon policy toward the Blacks. BYU is a Mormon school, owned and operated by The Church of Jesus Christ of Latter-day Saints.

Concerned, I sought out a member of the committee on the issue at the University to get more details. To my deep dismay, he said the issue had been active for about three years; that a research team had spent considerable time on the BYU campus; that several committees had studied the proposal; and as far as he knew, each committee had recommended a 'Do Pass' on the proposed action.

When I asked him if there was any effort from BYU or the LDS church to stop the action, he said, "Not to my knowledge. Perhaps they felt everything they could say had already been said." He was convinced the motion would easily pass when voted on.

With a heavy heart, I drove back to Mesa, wondering if anything could possibly be done at this late hour to prevent such a shameful action. As I drove near the church of a good pastor friend, an idea struck me. Maybe he would understand the gravity of this situation and write a letter in opposition to it. So I pulled into his driveway to find out.

His first comment was, "What is the matter with you today, Darl?" With some emotion, I blurted out, "I need a friend real bad." He responded, "You know I'm your friend. What can I do for you?" I explained the situation and asked if he could find it in his heart to write a letter to the ASU Faculty Senate asking them to refrain from such an unwise act.

Without answering, this honest man went to his typewriter. As he pecked away, I studied his face to guess what he was writing. Soon he pulled out the paper, handed it to me and said, "Get stationary from my secretary for this letter to the Faculty Senate, a copy for the President of ASU, one for the AD Hock committee, a copy for the President of BYU, one for your Stake President, a copy for you and one for me. Then bring the letters for my signature."

Quickly, I picked up the stationary from his secretary and climbed into my car. I could only drive a block, however, before I was overcome with curiosity to read what he had written. The letter struck hard at the integrity of a university that would meddle in the arena of religious doctrine. It emphatically made the point that it was not a proper academic role to judge theology, and then administer penalties to those who do not conform their theology to the academics' judgments.

I still feel the tremendous emotion of that moment—an abrupt change from feelings of near hopelessness to excited confidence. Nor can I forget the deep love I felt for that man who willingly put his professional reputation on the line for a friend who needed him.

Promptly, I had the letter typed and returned for his signature. As he walked with me to my car, he put his hand on my shoulder, and smiling said, "Darl, the millennium must be near. When a Lutheran pastor will go to bat to defend a Mormon's rights, the millennium has to be very close."

I went to seven other minister friends. Each one wrote a powerful letter to the University opposing their pending action. One letter declared that a great university cannot stoop to such behavior, for that would make it (the university) more bigoted than the Mormons were being accused of being. Such an action would not only compromise religious freedom, but academic freedom as well. Another wrote that he had lived among the Mormons for many years. It had been his observation that Mormons treated black people better than their non-Mormon neighbors did, so the issue was entirely one of theology, which was certainly not the concern of the University.

I have no doubt that the letters from these eight minister friends stopped the movement at Arizona State University to sever relations with Brigham Young University. To my knowledge, the proposed action was never brought to a vote by the Faculty Senate.

I appreciate those who sacrificed of themselves for my benefit as a Mormon, especially because that sacrifice brought no particular personal gain or recognition to them. My hope is that more members of the LDS church will become aware of, and appreciate the sacrifices made for their benefit by the religious leaders of other faiths.

To have a friend is to be a friend and to appreciate what he does for you. Love and friendship reward themselves, and if we show love and friendship, our bread, cast on the water, will return many fold; the sweet reward of true friends. I still feel deep emotion and love for wonderful ministers who so honestly practice the Gold Rule toward the Mormons.

❖

CHAPTER 9

The Golden Rule in Action

There were feelings of emotion in our discussions of the LDS Church being involved with the Arizona Ecumenical Council (AEC). A wonderful Baptist minister, Dr. Paul was doing his best as Executive Director to create a united effort among Christian churches for better moral and ethical behavior among our youth.

During many previous years, issues such politics and gender had prevented LDS involvement with the AEC, so we were not members of that council, but LDS activity and assistance to strengthen families and youth had been desired. The problem was, how could this take place when "part time" membership in AEC was not desired by either party.

Our discussions also included the possibility of *non-Christian* religions helping in projects to lift common moral and ethical values. I suggested to Dr. Paul that *he* could imagine the Lord weeping when those who proclaim His teachings of love and charity act like opponents or religious street gangs toward each other.

Since Dr. Paul was the Executive Director of AEC, his influence spread all over the State of Arizona. It gave him capacity to sponsor meetings to share common spiritual values. Surely the creator we all worship would want him to do that. So the burden was on his shoulders to give it a try.

With a beautiful spirit and determination, Dr. Paul assembled a group which became known as the InterFaith Action Coalition of Arizona (IFACA). Early discussions among this group had some tender challenges. When we met as strangers, and expressed our religious concepts that were not familiar to each other, and often used words with different meanings to explain and defend them, the risk of disrespect and offense of others was present, but when we came to realize that each religion professed a version of that precious jewel called the Golden Rule, a simple miracle seemed to bless our discussions. It beautifully turned our concerns for others more than for ourselves. It gently helped our problems become assets for service.

The Golden Rule created a deeper respect for each other. To realize that we would probably have another's brand of faith had we been raised in their home was jolting, and the goal to sincerely support each other in our common moral, ethical and spiritual virtues was inspiring because many were nearly the same.

Another pressing problem raised its head. "Who should join, or be allowed to belong to the InterFaith Action Coalition"? Some groups questioned why they had not been included. The profound answer was found The Golden Rule. IFACA was created for those who wanted to serve others – not themselves. Those who would not eagerly promote the practice of The Golden Rule would not feel very comfortable there.

Various small events were held where we became better acquainted with each other, and the faiths that each of us professed. These retreats helped us build strong bonds of friendship and respect as we studied together, ate together, and yes, even prayed together - each in our own way.

What a joy it was to hear a Rabbi respond when he was asked if it was offensive to him to hear us pray "in the name of Jesus Christ", that it had been initially, but now he realized that "that's just the way you pray"! He has become a dear friend and we have shared many wonderful moments together.

As the group grew, we also developed more "faith" in our organization, and yes, even a little bravery. We decided that we needed to demonstrate this unity to others, and scheduled an evening we called "The Faces of Faith" at a large hotel in downtown Phoenix. Each Faith Group was given about 20 minutes of public time to discuss their faith, and who they were. Information tables were set up, and about 700 chairs were in place to handle "the crowd". My the room looked empty and large as we jointly prayed for success that evening.

A large advertising campaign that included radio, television and print media - all at no cost to our impoverished organization - had been used to invite the public, but we had no idea who might come. To top it off, it was held early in the evening in August - the hottest month of the year - and was scheduled to last about 3 hours. (When you have 9 spokesmen for 9 religions, it takes a while).

As the appointed hour arrived, the staff of the hotel began to add more chairs to those already in place. What a joy to see nearly 1200 people participate in a wonderfully spiritual evening of sharing feelings of love. It was truly an example of The Golden Rule in action, and has lead to other similar events.

CHAPTER 10

LDS Sermon From A Protestant Pulpit?

I had been asked to give a "Mormon point of view" about lesson topics to a small class of young married people in a Protestant Sunday School. Arriving at the appointed time, I found the classroom empty except for the teacher who asked if I would mind giving my presentation in the chapel. I agreed, but panic threatened me when I saw the large chapel nearly filled with many classes of the Sunday School. My minister friend strolled in, quipping that he had "come to protect me" and that I had "45 minutes to tell all about Mormonism, so go for it."

In such moments, prayer comes naturally and quick. What should I say to those young and old, learned and unlearned, friend and foe, all at the same time? The answer was that I should first make these introductory points:

1. Every one of you is here in this church because of what you feel is right, good and beautiful. If anyone would conclude that you were committed in this church to something wrong, bad or ugly, you would

think he had neither charity nor good sense. That is about the way I feel about my commitment to my own church

2. My faith, like most others, may be compared to a picture on a jig saw puzzle. It is made up of many pieces—doctrines, beliefs, concepts and feelings. When the pieces are properly fitted together, it makes a beautiful and meaningful picture to me. Each piece adds dimension to the whole. As with the jig saw picture, it is impossible to look at just a few of the pieces and see the full meaning. Not many of us have the right attitude or desire to take the time to put enough pieces together to make an accurate judgment of another's faith.

3. Had I been raised and taught in your home as you were, I would probably now have the same religion you have. So also, had you been raised and taught in my home as I was, you would probably now follow the same religious faith that I do.

4. Since each person is motivated by the beauty and inspiration he sees and feels in his own faith, it is impossible for us to ever understand either a person or his faith unless we see and feel the beauty and inspiration he sees and feels. Without it, we pursue a path of ignorance and futility when we judge another's faith. The Lord said, "Don't do it."

5. Now, maybe my ability to recognize beauty and truth is about the same as yours. Since my faith is a most treasured possession, if my explanations don't appear to be beautiful and truthful to you, you can be very sure that you do not understand me. So please, all of you, listen with a positive, constructive attitude.

6. Some may question, "Who is a Christian?" Does a Christian keep the great commandment to love his neighbor as himself? Anyway, we all like those who act like Christians.

7. Since the Lord hears and answers prayers, please pray now for me to say the right words so you can feel the Lord's Spirit. If I fail, maybe you didn't pray hard enough.
8. If I would like to know the beauties of your faith, should I ask an antagonist against your faith to tell me about it, or should I ask you? Thanks for asking me to share with you the beauties of my faith. I sincerely hope that you can appreciate them."

Those points were the best I could think of to help them feel the attitude and the spirit of the golden Rule. The balance of my presentation was quite well received by that house full of Lutherans. I still feel a lot of love when I am with many of them.

CHAPTER 11

On Whose Side Am I?

Small groups of 'anti-Mormon' agitators traveled far to demonstrate and hand out literature against the LDS to the crowds at the pageant in Palmyra, New York. One of the local activists, Ross, discussed their activities with me. In seeming innocence, he acted surprised that the LDS resented his presence at the pageant.

He related several incidents as examples: A Boy Scout with a horn had blasted it right in his ear; other young people would go to each 'anti' available, get all the free 'anti' literature possible, then chuck it in the waste containers; another 'anti' was surrounded by three young people so he couldn't hand out literature and talk to pageant visitors.

I tried to help him recognize the simple fact that 'anti' attacks on a Mormon's cherished faith are much like attacks on his mother, his wife or the America that he loves. Is it possible that the 'antis' don't realize this? How could I help them see it?

The scripture in Galations 5th chapter seemed to fit, so I arranged the following sheet, "On Whose Side Am I?" and gave it to Ross. He responded with anger at the perceived suggestion that he was on Satan's side. He quickly informed me that

On Whose Side Am I?
Clarified in Galations 5:15-26

Jesus *"Fruits of the Spirit"*	**Satan** *"Lusts of the Flesh"*
By love serve one another	Bite and Devour one another
Friend	Antagonist
Peace	Strife
Goodwill	Ill will
Long Suffering, Kindness	Critical, Fault Finding
Goodness, Gentleness	Provoke one another
Joy	Misery
Forgiveness	Condemning
Meekness	Vain Glory
Lead by the Spirit	Evil Nature
Love thy neighbor as thyself	Hatred, Fighting, Dissension
They are Christ's Gal. 5:21	***They which do such things shall not inherit the Kingdom of God*** Gal. 5:21

Arranged by Darl Andersen

the Mormons were those on Satan's side and that the Mormons had better consider their own behavior. I was happy to suggest that he and the Lord would be his judge, not me. The sheet was what the scripture said for all and I thanked him for his honest opinion.

As I carefully read Galatians, chapter five again from Ross' point of view and from the perspective of his attitude, it appeared that I, and perhaps a few other LDS I know, sometimes appear to be on Satan's side. This is of much greater concern for me than what Ross does. The message of the Book of Mormon (Moroni 7:14) explains as clearly as the difference between daylight and dark night, just whose side anyone is on:

"Wherefore, take heed, my beloved brethren, (faithful members of the Church), that ye do not judge that which is evil to be of God, or that which is good and of God to be of the devil. For behold, my brethren, it is given unto you to judge, that ye may know good from evil; and the way to judge is as plain, that ye may know with a perfect knowledge, as the daylight is from the dark night. For behold, the Spirit of Christ is given to every man, that he may know good from evil; wherefore, I show unto you the way to judge; for every thing which inviteth to do good, and to persuade to believe in Christ, is sent forth by the power and gift of Christ; wherefore ye may know with a perfect knowledge it is of God. But whatsoever thing persuadeth men to do evil, and believe not in Christ, and deny him, and serve not God, then ye may know with a perfect knowledge it is of the devil..." (Moroni 7:14-17)

Often those who have committed their hearts and their lives to teaching people to believe in Jesus Christ and keep the Lord's commandments are judged to be evil and of the devil because they teach a "different" interpretation of scripture and doctrine. On the other hand, those who spend their lives and energies fault finding, accusing and condemning their neighbors may be judged to be good and of God simply because they appear to interpret the scriptures "correctly", as we do.

Indeed there are those who evidently do not understand the difference between the ways of Jesus Christ and the ways of Satan, for some preach Christ yet act like the adversary. That seems nearly impossible.

The diagram entitled "On Whose Side Am I?" uses words from different biblical translations of Galatians 5:15-26 in the New Testament. It can help us to more clearly distinguish the Lord's side from Satan's side. For sometimes we may be on the wrong side and not even realize whose side we are on.

What a precious jewel the Golden Rule is. "Do for others what you would have them do for you." It peacefully guides us away from the most painful reality that sometimes we act like the adversary but think we follow the Lord. Heaven help us to more faithfully live the Golden Rule.

CHAPTER 12

Minister's Children Join LDS Church

A minister friend was a very charitable man, noticeably so toward the religious faith of his neighbors. So it was quite natural for his children to enroll in LDS Seminary classes with their friends at the high school. In that environment, they developed a desire to join the LDS church. The parents suggested that they should wait until they were more mature, at least until they were of legal age, before they made such a religious commitment. But when that time arrived, the children were still of the same conviction, and after they had taken the regular missionary lessons, a date was set for their baptism to become members of the LDS Church.

Because of my close association and deep respect for this minister, I felt some of the pain and difficulty I knew was his. So, in concern, I called him for a lunch date where we could visit and he could talk about his pent up emotions. He came right in.

Trying to ease the distress he felt, I asked if he could describe what it was that hurt him most. He mentioned two major points. First, he said that in changing their religion, the kids had completely rejected the beautiful faith and beliefs that he, as their father and minister, had carefully taught them. Second, acceptance of Mormonism was an insult and slap in the face to their parents, and it made him feel a little bitter. In no way would he have anything to do with his kids in connection with the Mormons.

Since I knew he had some very special children, so full of love and honesty that they would never want to hurt or offend their parents in any way, I asked if it might help if I addressed his hurts from a different point of view.

With his approval, I expressed these ideas to him:

"Point one: Within your church's theological structure, there is considerable latitude to accommodate individual opinion. Right or wrong, probably your children honestly feel they have rejected none of the beauty and faith taught by their parents. They have found what they feel is additional exciting evidence of the truths in the scriptures. They have gained added understanding of the meaning and purpose of life. They have experienced a personal witness of the spirit to support their faith that Jesus Christ is truly their Lord and Savior. In their minds, they are expanding the beauty and strength of their faith."

"Point two: Religious feelings run deep and tender, but suppose your kids had gone the way of crime, become drug addicts, traveled the sex route or displayed hatred and contempt for their parents. Then you would have real heartache. But on the contrary, your kids have taken the most honorable and right course they understand. They have followed their most noble impulses, despite opposition from those they love. They have had the strength to maintain their integrity and clear consciences before their Father in Heaven. No doubt your children have a deeper love for their parents now than ever before."

"As parents, you can be so proud to have children with such outstanding virtues. Perhaps there are thousands of parents in this town who would be willing to give most anything they have if they could trade places with you regarding the behavior of their children. And, I suppose, had you been raised and taught in my home, you would feel that what your children have done is the most wonderful thing that could happen to them."

As we parted, we both felt much better and very fortunate.

He did attend their baptism. He even spoke at his son's missionary farewell. The family has remained close and united, and they have been such a delightful example of love, charity, and respect in a family which has members of different religious faiths.

CHAPTER 13

Parallel Positions to Protestant Points

Attending Sunday School classes in different churches is an educational and enjoyable experience—usually. But at one church, I discovered that the 'Concerned Christians' had presented their anti-Mormon distortions during the previous two class periods. Several of their group were in the class again that morning. The minister invited me to answer their accusations rather than give a lecture or a sermon.

Though I did my best, the spirit in the class was quite negative and ugly. Near the end, I commented that it seemed to me the reason for Sunday School was to learn of the Lord, to be inspired by His spirit, and to unitedly strengthen our personal commitments to Him. Surely, Christians should love each other, help and strengthen each other and look for the positive and good in each other rather than find fault, ridicule and condemn. I said I felt badly to have participated in a class that had failed to reach any of these desired goals. I apologized to them for participating in a discussion when the Lord's spirit was so evasive.

A good man in the class, whom I had known for many years, responded. "Darl, we hear what you are saying. We know the Mormons quite well. You are good neighbors, honorable community leaders and you have outstanding families. We would like to love you, but you won't let us. When you go around saying that we don't teach the truth in our Church, that we don't have divine authority, and that our baptisms are not acceptable to the Lord, then we just can't love you. If you would quit saying those things, it would help a lot."

When I asked him if he thought Mormons taught the truth or had the authority to perform a baptism acceptable to the Lord, his answer was definite. "No, you don't".

So I suggested that sometimes we condemn and refuse to love each other for doing the same things that we do ourselves.

He quickly replied, "But with you Mormons, it is different. Your prophet, Joseph Smith, said that only the Mormon Church was right, and that all other churches were wrong".

I asked him if that wasn't the same justification the founders of his church used when they organized it. If not, why didn't they just join with the Methodists, Presbyterians, Lutherans or some other existing church? In fact, almost every church was organized because its founders felt that existing churches were not right in some way or another. Though other founders may have used different words of explanation than Joseph Smith did, still some of the basic reasons were about the same.

Those with an adversary spirit have found faults with every faith. Even Jesus Christ was crucified because of the accusations of his adversaries. Since, we all have many faults, could there be a heaven if the Lord was a faultfinder with an adversary spirit?

I concluded that we should be more careful how we judge each other. We may be acting like hypocrites in the eyes of the Lord when we condemn others for the same things we do ourselves.

When my minister friend showed me to the door, I realized I had hurt him by inferring to members of his congregation that he was acting hypocritically by his criticism of the Mormons. I felt badly that I had done that. However, although it was an unpleasant experience for both of us, I believe it helped us both to understand more clearly that followers of the Master must indulge less in unkind judgments and more in charity toward each other.

CHAPTER 14

Impossible to Know How He Did It

From all over the world, some of the most interesting people come to visit the Grandin Press Building in Palmyra, N.Y. It is the place where the Book of Mormon was first printed. Recently, two sharp looking college professors came in. One man, who taught languages in a leading university, said he was a "student of the Restoration". He was not a Mormon, but his hobby was a study of the amazing process of the establishment of Mormonism. His study stopped at the Mississippi River, he said. It didn't follow the Mormons west.

During his tour of the Grandin Building, this alert man made comments which convinced me that he knew much more about the historic details of the restoration of the Church of Jesus Christ of Latter-day Saints than I did. Most of his comments were gentle, intellectual questions about the 'divine claims of Joseph Smith'.

At one point, this astute scholar asked if I was aware that a rather reliable source had reported that some of the translation of the Book of Mormon was done by using the Urim &

Thummim when the gold plates were not present. "Then," he wondered, "if that were true, would it cast some question on the integrity of the Book of Mormon?"

My response was that I didn't know how the translation was done by using the Urim & Thummim even when the gold plates were present. But, to me, just as with the Bible, the real test of the Book of Mormon is to be found in its content, not in the process of translation. Did the fact that Moses wrote the story of the creation some 2500 years after he said it happened, and apparently with no written record of those events, cast doubt on the integrity of the Bible so far as the professor was concerned?

The professor answered that he didn't know whether he believed the Bible either.

Later in the tour presentation, I commented, "In my opinion, any reasonable, honest person who becomes aware of the amazing accomplishments of Joseph Smith, and comes to know of the qualities of his personality will gain a tremendous respect and appreciation for the man—especially if the divine influence in his accomplishments is not accepted."

"And you know Joseph Smith very well," I said to him.

The professor then made this surprising statement: "Let me tell you what I think about Joseph Smith. Do you realize that Joseph Smith was the most profound theologian the world has ever known? Nowhere in all history is there a theology that compares with his for meaning, beauty, simplicity and cohesion. At the same time, it is powerful, convincing and satisfying to those who believe."

My response was that the Lord Jesus Christ was the greatest theologian.

He said, "The Lord didn't write anything. Everything that He spoke has come to us through the mind and words of someone else written many years later."

After thanking him for his keen insight, I suggested that many other contributions made by Joseph Smith were also significant. He organized converts from many varied backgrounds into a remarkable society. Though persecuted and driven from state to state, his people rapidly built cities, schools and temples and established commerce. He even prepared to run for president of the United States. How could this "unlearned youth", who was martyred in a jail at the age of 38, possibly have accomplished all this, and at the same time, produce three volumes which are accepted by over six million Mormons as being sacred scripture?

The professor answered simply, "It is impossible to comprehend the psychological process by which Joseph Smith accomplished what he did."

We were in near agreement on that statement. The difference was, Mormons add divine influence to that process, just as divine influence explains the accomplishments of other great prophets whose works are recorded in the Bible.

CHAPTER 15

How Did the Book of Mormon Get Printed?

Pastor H. was perhaps the most forthright minister I had known. Of German decent and staunch Lutheran faith, he was inclined to "lay it on the line" about his beliefs and conclusions to the matter. Our dialogue, therefore, was rather blunt. He still refers to our early discussions as being "bloody". So do I.

My first impression of him was that he was an honest man. This not only caused me to respect him, but it also convinced me that he would respect my sincere faith, if he could just come to understand it a little. Our first four sessions together each lasted over an hour. Our communications were straight to the point as he 'told me every error of Mormonism.'

A typical example of our dialogue was his sharp criticism of the Book of Mormon. He questioned "how anyone could possibly believe a book to be divine that has had over 5000 changes made in it from the first printed edition to the one now in use."

My response was that the changes were mostly punctuation

and structure, such as arranging the text into verses and paragraphs for easy referral, much like the Bible. I said that in my opinion, these were not significant or meaningful changes.

With this, he strongly disagreed. "In Christian honesty, you should know that it is impossible to make 5000 changes without causing significant changes in meaning." he said. He concluded that the integrity of the book had to have been affected.

At that moment, I noticed his own well-used Bible lying on his desk between us. It was a new revised edition, so I commented that perhaps most of the words in his Bible had been changed during his lifetime. If that circumstance was acceptable to him, he should not question LDS "Christian honesty."

Neither of us was then aware that the first manuscript of the Book of Mormon, written by Oliver Cowdery as he took dictation from Joseph Smith, had hardly any punctuation at all. I have since learned this fact from the photographic copies of the original manuscript which are in a display case at the Grandin Press building in Palmyra, New York. Even when he wrote by hand a second copy (to take to the printer, a few pages at a time), it is apparent that Oliver Cowdery did not address the challenge of punctuation.

Viewing these early manuscripts indicates to me: 1) That Oliver Cowdery was writing down rapid dictation with no punctuation being dictated. Most of the 522 page book was written in about 65 days; 2) That perhaps the engravings on the Book of Mormon plates did not contain an equivalent of the kind of punctuation one uses when writing in English; 3) That the task at hand for Joseph Smith and Oliver Cowdery was to translate and write down the translation of a record, not to write a book. Had the intent been to write a book, school teacher Cowdery would have certainly tried to punctuate it; 4) That what Oliver Cowdery wrote was not simply the copying of some other writing. Had it been a copy, he probably would have copied the punctuation also; 5) That a very capable type-setter by the name of John Gilbert, who was not a Mormon, was hired by the publisher, E.B. Grandin, to add punctuation, make a few grammatical corrections, and create a book from the manuscript Joseph Smith and Oliver Cowdery provided.

Imagine the challenge of punctuating profound scripture the way the Lord would want it done—a heavy responsibility!

The Grandin Building display shows each of the few simple steps that have occurred in the development of the present edition of the Book of Mormon. They appear so open, honest and unpretentious to me. I wondered how large a display it would take to show all of the steps in the development of a modern edition of the Bible. I wished these steps could have been as few, simple, open, honest and unpretentious as those for the development of the Book of Mormon, and that the divine influence in the translation process could have been as evident.

❖

CHAPTER 16

How Can I Believe the Book of Mormon?

Many beautiful Christian people attend Sunday School classes to study the Bible, learn of the Lord and enjoy His spirit. In such a Protestant class, a delightful woman turned to me, a visiting Mormon, and asked a very honest question: "How can you possibly believe the Book of Mormon to be scripture comparable to the Holy Bible?"

Since new religious concepts are difficult to accept, I wanted to relate my answer to the concepts she already accepted, so I asked her how she knew the New Testament was scripture.

This gracious lady stated that she had not always believed the Bible, but because of difficult problems in her life, she had come to really want to know if it was true. In her attempt to find out, she said she had taken the following steps: 1) She carefully studied the Bible. 2) She thoughtfully considered its contents and message. 3) She sincerely prayed for divine help to know if it was true. After repeating these steps a few times, she said, a sweet feeling of peaceful assurance came over her. She was convinced that those who wrote the Bible were humble servants of the Lord inspired to write divine messages from God for our individual peace and benefit. Though there were some physical evidences to support the truth of the Bible, it was this feeling of peaceful assurance that had given her conviction of its divine message.

When I asked if taking those same steps could be used by others to gain an assurance that the Bible is the word of God, the members of the class seemed to agree that they could, and many had.

I assured them that I had a deep conviction that the Bible is the word of God. Those steps had worked just as well for me as for them.

So also, by following those same steps, I have come to know that the Book of Mormon is the word of God. And by those same steps, millions of others have come to the same conviction; namely, that those who wrote the book of Mormon were humble servants of the Lord inspired to write divine messages from God for our peace and benefit.

I said that following those steps with respect to the Book of Mormon produces the same conviction of the truth and value of the Book of Mormon as they do of the truth and value of the Bible.

There are many who do not believe the Bible to be the word of God. This is not so much because of the contents of the book, but because of the attitude of people and their unwillingness to take the necessary steps to gain the feeling for themselves that it is true. It seems that anyone who believes the Bible can come to believe the Book of Mormon if they have the same attitude and take the same steps that led them to believe the Bible. They can receive that same peaceful, satisfying assurance.

Another class member then asked, "Why is there a need for the Book of Mormon anyway? Isn't the Bible all we need?"

My answer was that, to me, it is like asking, "Why is there a need for the gospels of Luke and John? Why four gospels? Why do we need all these epistles of the Apostle Paul?" Or, "Why do we need preachers to tell us what they think? Isn't the Bible all we need?

To those who believe it, the Book of Mormon is a tremendous source of faith, testimony, joy and understanding of Jesus Christ. Personally, I feel so very fortunate and blessed to have a conviction of the truth of the Book of Mormon, in addition to the Bible.

CHAPTER 17

Similarities: Apostle Paul and Joseph Smith

Palmyra, New York is quite a small township with only a few ministers. Part of our missionary assignment was to be helpful friends with religious leaders and to spread love and good will among them. This was a pleasant opportunity. Sending them 'candy bar greeting cards', attending their special programs, and having lunch with them was quite rewarding.

During a lunch conversation with them one day, we had a relaxed conversation about Joseph Smith whose amazing claim of being a 'Prophet of God' had started right there. Their very honest and sincere questions of how LDS thinking could bring such conclusions were pressing. The simplest answers I could find were by using concepts with which they were well acquainted. The dialogue developed in the following way.

The foundation for the religious faith of both Christians and Jews is found in their scriptures, the Bible. If a person believes that the Old Testament and the New Testament are sacred scripture, written by men inspired of God, it is usually the result of family faith and tradition. But the content of the scripture is used as evidence to establish the divine calling of those who wrote it (that the writer was inspired of God to write). As a tree is measured by its fruit, so a writer is measured by the content of his writings.

As a specific example, consider the Apostle Paul who wrote much of the New Testament. Although Paul was a learned man, Christians believe he could not have written what he wrote without divine help. What he wrote is considered to be of greater truth and inspiration than the best he could have possibly written by his own natural abilities. Christians are convinced that the truth and inspiration in Paul's writings came by the gift and power of God.

Paul's writings are not only evidence that he received inspiration from Heaven, but they are also evidence that Paul had a divine vision which completely turned his life around from being a persecutor of Christians to becoming the great missionary for Jesus Christ.

Now in the same way, what is written in the Book of Mormon is the measure of the divine calling of those who wrote it. It is also a specific evidence that Joseph Smith translated the record from which it came by the gift and power of God as surely as the Apostle Paul wrote by the gift and power of God. It would be utterly impossible for an unlearned youth—or any other person—to produce a book that could so powerfully impact the lives of so many millions of people as the Book of Mormon has done, without divine help.

Likewise, this book is evidence that Joseph Smith had a divine vision—much like Paul—which completely transformed his life from being an unlearned youth, to becoming the greatest witness and missionary for Jesus Christ in this day. The very purpose of the Book of Mormon, as well as the life of Joseph Smith, is to proclaim Jesus Christ as Lord.

Many of the writings of both the Apostle Paul and Joseph Smith became scripture to believers, building tremendous commitment and dedication among them. Though the Apostle Paul and Joseph Smith were persecuted and driven, and though both of them eventually lost their lives, still the church which each espoused grew across the world. This happened because believers accepted Paul and Joseph Smith to be apostles and prophets of God, with the divine mission to proclaim Jesus Christ as Savior to all the world.

Many millions of people do not believe the Old Testament, or the New Testament, or the Book of Mormon to be scripture or inspired writings from God. Usually, the reason is they do not know the contents of the books nor have they felt inspiration from carefully reading their pages. Perhaps others have a negative attitude toward the books which shut out beauty and inspiration.

But the great numbers who do believe are convinced there is sufficient evidence to convince rational minds that these books were written by divine inspiration for the good and blessing of needy mortals. Belief usually comes to a person with a positive attitude who will take a few simple steps:

1) Have a real desire to know if the writings are inspired and true.
2) Read carefully and thoughtfully.
3) Ponder and consider the contents.
4) Pray humbly to God for His help to know if the record is from Him.

This process which brings a personal conviction of divine origin works equally well for all three of these books of scripture. It has brought deep conviction and commitment to many multitudes who have tried it.

By this process, a person may come to know with equal certainty:

a) that Moses is a prophet measured by the Old Testament,
b) that Paul is a prophet measured by the New Testament, and
c) that Joseph Smith is a prophet measured by the Book of Mormon.

CHAPTER 18

Living Prophets

Carefully, I listened as three minister friends explained their deep feelings and convictions about prophets. They concluded with these points.
1) Jesus Christ was the last great prophet.
2) There is no need for prophets today because the Bible contains all the information necessary for salvation.
3) It is evil to now claim living prophets.

They then asked for my response to their positions.

First I thanked them sincerely for sharing their convictions and reasoning with me. Then I suggested we might understand each other better by noting parallels between our beliefs such as:
1) We all believe in answers to prayer.
2) We all believe we can receive inspiration from the Lord.
3) We are all convinced that the Lord gives us direction as we serve Him and our neighbors.

"There are many definitions of the term 'prophet.' You may use one and I may use another. To help gain understanding, we need to use the same definition. For example, in my dictionary at home, the first two definitions of a prophet are: 1) One who speaks or acts for God, and 2) One who speaks or acts by divine inspiration. According to both of these definitions," I said, "would each of us be a prophet? If we don't speak or act for God, who do we speak or act for? If we don't speak or act under divine inspiration, under what inspiration do we speak or act?"

They responded to the humor of the question.

Thoughtfully, I continued. "Does the divine inspiration given to a prophet as he serves God come from the same source as the divine inspiration that we claim comes to us when we serve God? How can we clearly draw a line between a prophet, and a person who is not quite a prophet? Is it the amount of inspiration received? Is it the ecclesiastical position held by the one receiving the inspiration? Is it some specific calling or assignment from the Lord?

"Mormon Christians believe that the Lord personally directed the establishment of the Church of Jesus Christ of Latter-day Saints, and still directs it. For the Mormon, that person to whom the Lord gives specific instruction for the functioning of His Church is called a prophet, comparable to Peter, James and John, Christ's ancient apostles. LDS also believe that those same persons, Peter, James and John, personally conferred authority on Joseph Smith and Oliver Cowdery to perform the ordinances and functions of the Savior's restored church—quite a specific assignment and an overwhelming responsibility.

"It appears that you men see no need for the specific direction and authorization of a prophet in what you say and do. To each of you, your church is one among many churches which honor, proclaim and teach of the Savior, but you evidently feel you have the confirmation of the Spirit to say and do what you say and do.

"Few believe in living prophets, and some are offended because others do, but it is exciting to consider the desirable benefits which come from being led by a living prophet. Some of these benefits are an increase of peace in the believer's heart, purpose in his life, joy in his living, closeness to his God, and greater conviction of the divine mission of Jesus Christ." I said.

"Evidence of these benefits is found in increased commitment and response among Mormon Christians, their missionary zeal, their welfare program, an unpaid clergy and a relatively happy and charitable people. These are just a few of the noticeable benefits.

"Really, wouldn't it be just exciting to have living prophets like Peter, James and John among us? Doesn't our society need them today as much as in New Testament times? Probably, deep down, every sincere Christian would wish it could be so."

❖

CHAPTER 19

A Prophet, Key to Sacrifice

Among religious leaders there seems to be an ever present curiosity and concern about the apparent sacrifice that LDS Church members make for their faith. Many minister friends have personally asked me for dimensions and understanding of these noticeable qualities. They often ask: From what source comes the dedication to carry out a tremendous welfare program that cares for the physical needs of church members? What is the motivation that causes so much participation by men in their Priesthood activities or by women in Relief Society involvement? How do the youth develop a commitment to be active in seminary and institute instruction? And particularly, what moves them to fill missions for their church where they "pay their own way?"

One such clergyman was quite knowledgeable of LDS doctrine and teachings. He recognized a warm spirit of brotherhood and unity so enjoyed by church members. Though he had a deep respect for many of the programs and practices unique to Mormonism, he could not agree at all with LDS claims to "Exclusive Authority", as he called it. He said, "God may speak through most any church leader of most any denomination in that denomination's own structure of authority."

This minister knew that Mormon Christians believe each person is entitled to receive divine direction concerning his own problems and responsibilities, and to find answers to his own prayers, but that the one who receives divine direction for the Church of Jesus Christ is a prophet

The Mormon concept that Jesus Christ has A Church – His Church – which He directs through a living prophet with "exclusive Priesthood authority" was unacceptable to this minister.

One day this clergyman expressed to me his desire to know how to build deep dedication among the youth in his church like that demonstrated among Mormon youth such as their willingness to accept a 'call on a mission'. How could this be done, he wondered.

This seemed like an appropriate time and setting to consider a living prophet. My comment to him was that it seemed he could never get such a commitment from the youth or adults in his church until they felt the authority which called them to sacrifice was from a higher source than their minister or a committee of their equals in the church. When individuals clearly feel that the call to sacrifice is from God, they will eagerly respond.

The concept of a prophet at the head of a church who has divine authority and receives divine direction to "call" individuals to positions is a way to persuade people to give of themselves. Though we may resist accepting the principle of "exclusive authority", we can still recognize its effectiveness and great power.

We might ponder the question: "If our Father in Heaven wants dedication and commitment to His purposes from us, would He want to have us feel that the call we receive comes from Him. The truism that "You can't have the fruit without the roots," seems to apply here. The desired "fruit" is a deep conviction and dedication to the cause of the Lord. The "roots" refers to the personal assurance that God speaks in a direct way through a prophet, or to his representative in leadership, who "calls" us to service and sacrifice.

❖

CHAPTER 20

Who Is of the Apostasy?

Some in the clergy group were castigating the Church of Jesus Christ of Latter-day Saints because they felt the church taught that 'Clergymen are of the apostasy, and totally without God's truth and authority.' To help them understand and feel better, I walked with them, step by step, through my Mormon belief about the apostasy. When I finished, they had disagreed with only the last point, and they went away with more understanding of and charity for the Mormon belief in an "apostasy."

These are the steps:

1) Apostasy means a departure from religious principles; a lack of comprehension by growing human minds and hearts.

2) Apostasy has been a natural re-occurring process throughout all of religious history. The apostasies at the times of Noah, Moses, and Jesus are very apparent examples.

3) As people have not learned His truth, God has sent prophets to clarify and restore His truth with authority. Biblical history indicates that this happened over and over again. Historically, only a comparative few

have readily accepted living prophets bringing revealed truth from God.

4) *The Savior taught His glorious gospel of love, which was a light to the world and the most lofty way of life ever known. It was to save the world from misery and bring abundant life. Jesus said, "I am the light of the world; he that followeth me shall not walk in darkness, but shall have the light of life." (John 8:12)*

5) The 'dark ages' occurred because the light of Christ was not followed. Surely, some of the 'way of the Lord' was simply lost. The leaders who led the world into the dark ages did not follow the way, the truth and the light that Jesus taught.

6) Most Christians agree that the religious teachings and practices during that period were the reason for the Great Reformation. Those religious teachings and practices were the basic reason for the protest, and the justification for the formation of many Protestant churches.

7) The Church of Jesus Christ of Latter-day Saints teaches that the great Reformers, those spiritual giants of wisdom, vision and integrity, were "men raised up by God," to perform very special and important missions.

8) Mormon Christians believe that without these great Reformers and the enlightenment their efforts brought about, Mormonism could not have been established. It took an atmosphere of religious freedom and tolerance to make possible the survival of a religious belief system based on the claim of new revealed truth from Heaven.

9) So, as Mormons believe, prophets speaking again today are but another glorious chapter in the oft repeated process of God revealing and clarifying truth with authority for the blessing of His children. Proph-

ets are a new evidence of God's love for, and tender mercies toward us. They are a precious new witness to the divinity of Jesus Christ and His beautiful Gospel. This is a message that brings peace, joy and enrichment to those who embrace it.

CHAPTER 21

Who Has the Lord's Gifts?

While talking at lunch with a most delightful and charitable Catholic Bishop, our dialogue brought into clear focus some sobering points.

Both the Roman Catholic Church and the Church of Jesus Christ of Latter-day Saints (as well as other churches) claim gifts of the Lord which are superior to those possessed by other denominations. Some of these gifts may be: 1) The Lord's church which He established and personally directs; 2) The Lord's authority to operate His church and perform His ordinances therein; 3) The Lord's truth in its most pure and correct condition; 4) The Lord's spirit, to be with and direct the leaders and members in the church.

How can an honest mind deal with this conflict? Can we conclude that the Lord's precious gifts of His church, His authority, His truth, and His spirit should make a noticeable difference in a church since the very purpose of His gifts is to produce desired fruits?

Can we observe the evidence, or fruits, the Lord expected of those who possess His gifts?

Does reason suggest that the gift of the Lord's church as directed by Him, would provide the most effective methods, pro-

grams and procedures to bring the rich fruits and blessings from the Lord to members of the church and all others? Should the presence of these fruits and blessings be evident to those who seek the Lord's church?

Among those who have the gift of the Lord's authority, would there be real leadership to administer, bless and share the light, truth and joy of His gospel? Would they not reach out to all people and give leadership to overcome ignorance, sin and apathy?

Should those who have the gift of the Lord's truth set an example of understanding and respect of others? Would they not be a most joyous and serving people who really try to love their neighbors as themselves and practice the Golden Rule?

Would those who possess the gift of the Lord's spirit be filled with the balm of charity, and go forth undaunted to bring peace and good will in a troubled world? Would the Spirit of the Master be apparent in their countenances?

Now if such results, or fruits, are not an evidence of the presence of the Lord's gifts, how can the gifts be recognized? Anyone may claim to have the gifts. Of what benefit are the gifts without the fruit? The Master said, "By their fruits ye shall know them." A good tree is known by its fruit.

The burden that falls on those who claim to have the Lord's gifts is a great one, for the fruits must be there to evidence the presence of the gifts. If someone had the gifts but did not produce their desirable fruits, would the Lord not relocate His gifts to a people among whom his desired fruits would be produced, for the purpose of the gifts is to produce desirable fruits, not the gratification of pride or ego.

Those with the gifts have the tremendous responsibility to be a "fertile field" where the gifts may take root, flourish and grow so that the desirable fruits may be produced abundantly. Of what value are the gifts but to bring fruits? Without fruits, the gifts condemn us.

CHAPTER 22

Temple Wedding – Parents Excluded

Mike's parents were not members of the LDS Church. They felt hurt with bitterness because they could not attend his wedding in the temple. The depth of their feelings caused a continuing barrier to happy family relationships. This broke Mike's heart because he wanted so much to be close to his parents and to share with them his most cherished feelings.

Twenty years later, when Mike asked me to perform the temple wedding of his daughter, he asked if there was any way possible for someone to talk with his parents 'in the temple.' He so hoped that someone might soften their hurt and bitter feelings.

Arrangements were made, and immediately after the wedding ceremony, I went to the temple foyer to talk with Mike's parents. Though the area was crowded, we found a corner for a short 'temple visit.'

I sincerely expressed my concern for the hurt they felt because they could not attend their granddaughter's wedding, and that I wished somehow they could share the inspirations of such a precious family ceremony. I tried to answer their questions and help them understand the value of the temple.

Then I told them a little story about my good pastor friend who had asked me to explain to him why he could not go into the temple. The Pastor asked, "Do you Mormons think you are better than I am? Do you assume the Lord loves you more than he loves me? Do you have some other excuse for refusing to let me in the Temple or are you just bigoted?"

My response to the Pastor was that he already knew the answer to his questions. He knew that in his own life there were sacred and personal experiences that he shared only with certain people—some with just his wife, some with his family, and some with only those who had the same faith and belief that he had.

Within the temple occurs a sacred and powerful worship service. For effectiveness, it is restricted to those who share the same faith and belief—somewhat as was the case with the temples of old. The goal is to lift and inspire those who enter to more completely love the Lord and keep His commandments. Its purpose is to encourage strong, united families with honorable fathers, lovely mothers and delightful children.

To those without the benefit that comes from a common faith and understanding, the symbolism used in the temple ceremony could be empty and negative. If the temple doors are opened to curiosity seekers and antagonists, the inspiration and blessings now found in the temple worship services would be restrained.

The Pastor responded by wondering why he hadn't thought of those answers himself. It seemed so simple.

I suggested that the temple doors would be open to him if he believed as Mormons do and lived the standards required of those who enter the temple.

After telling this story, I congratulated Mike's parents for raising such a fine son, for Mike is a good husband, the father of a precious family, and has an honorable reputation in the community.

His parents knew that the temple ceremony, along with his church, had made a strong impression for good on the life of their son.

Mike's parents expressed their thanks to me for the "words of understanding." That night at the reception, they again expressed appreciation. Later, Mike came to me with tears in his eyes. He choked as he said, "That is the first time in twenty years that anyone has been able to talk with my parents to ease their pain and help them see the beauties of my precious faith."

CHAPTER 23

The Endowment – A Gift of Understanding

Because Latter-day Saints don't talk outside the temple of things within it, anti-Mormons gladly fill the void with their unkind explanations of temple ceremonies. Clergymen, whose role is to provide information and answers to questions about religion, are forced into a corner. If they refuse to accept these unkind explanations, where can they find kind accurate ones? Surely, ministers deserve to have kind explanations available to them. How can we explain things we don't talk about so that honorable people can have needed answers?

Three clergy friends asked me one day if I could find a way to help them with a little explanation of the temple experience. Could I comfortably give them some kind of an overview? My efforts to help them went about like this:

"To me, the temple ceremony is a most powerful worship service. It helps people feel closer to Heaven and nearer to the angels than about anything I know of. The strongest bonds of family unity and strength are welded there. The admirable qualities you observe among LDS families are, to a large extent, a product of temple worship."

When they wondered how the temple achieves those benefits, I suggested that it was by teaching correct principles. "Part of the temple service is an endowment which I like to view as a gift of understanding of life's meaning—one of the most precious gifts a loving Father in Heaven can give to us, his children.

"Much of the endowment ceremony is a drama. In this drama, through the use of symbolism and the spoken word, there is presented, by analogy, a meaningful picture of our eternal relationships. Understanding is given to us about our relationship to our Father in Heaven; our relationship to our Lord and Savior, Jesus Christ; our relationship to time and to eternity; our relationship to the experience of life; our relationship to our families and to each other.

"This picture of the eternal relationships in our lives may be compared to the picture typically found on a box containing a jigsaw puzzle. Just as this picture becomes a guide to those who put the pieces of the jigsaw puzzle together, so also the picture of eternal relationships received in the Temple becomes a guide to help us put the pieces of our lives together. Just as the pieces of a jigsaw puzzle have purpose, meaning and beauty when fit into the whole picture, so also do the pieces—the experiences—of our lives have purpose, meaning and beauty when fit into the whole picture of our eternal relationships. That picture, then, is a gift of understanding.

"Another good analogy may be the multiplication tables. I recall a time when, as a lad in the primary grade, we were about to have a test in arithmetic. I was repeatedly reciting through the house, 'four times four equals sixteen.'

"My father recognized my problem and asked, ' Son, do you know why four times four equals sixteen?' Then he showed me with his fingers the reason why four times four equaled sixteen.

"What a wonderful help! Now I didn't have to rely just on memory. I could reason it out. But even more exciting than that, I could also figure out that three times four equaled twelve, that five times four equaled twenty, etc. Knowing the 'reason why' gave me understanding of arithmetic."

An example of how understanding enhances spiritual concepts comes from John Heidenreich, our daughter's father-in-law. John was by nature a sensitive, spiritual and scholarly man who serviced 25 years as a Protestant minister. In his life history, he mentions that often, during his ministry, he had a yearning to explore, in discussion, the deeper spiritual topics of the gospel.

But, he said, he found little satisfaction. Whenever he sought out discussion with other clergy, they seemed to him to have a learned theology based on a profession of faith, and not very discussible. When he approached members of his own congregation, they said that theology was not their profession, and they did not know about such things.

John's teenage son, Fred, had a curious and inquiring mind. One day Fred came home bringing two Mormon missionaries because he thought his father would like to hear their unique and rational theology.

To John, these missionaries at first appeared to be "nineteen-year-old kids, barely dry behind the ears, with no professional theological training." To John's amazement, these "kids" seemed eager to discuss the deeper spiritual implications of the gospel. Later, another set of missionaries came to his home, and these, he said, "just wouldn't stop talking about theological topics." In his history, he then raises the question—without giving an answer, "What is so unique about nearly all Mormons, though they are without theological schooling, yet they are open and eager for deep theological discussion?"

One answer to John's question is that even without theological schooling, the rational theology of the LDS Church gives them a depth of understanding beyond memorized concepts or scriptures—a gift given them most effectively through the Temple endowment. This understanding is a real help as each person seeks answers to life's most significant challenges, such as: -the meaning and purpose of life, -our relationship with God and the Savior, -how to find joy and the abundant life, -why and how to live more Christ-like, -how to feel closer to Him, -why and how families, the source of life's greatest joys can be forever, and -how to find peace in our hearts and purpose in our living.

The temple endowment is a divine gift of understanding.

CHAPTER 24

Do Mormons Believe In a Physical God?

At the last meeting in a series of Methodist study classes on Mormonism, a good Methodist named Ray emotionally stated: "I have lived among the Mormons for many years. They are good neighbors with fine families and they serve well in the community, but I am unable to accept them as Christians because they believe in a physical God."

That statement troubled me a lot. Is the Mormon concept of God that much more "physical" than the Methodist concept? Why would Ray wish to exclude Mormons from the category of "Christians?" So the next day I called on Ray's minister, Rev. Don, for help in understanding his statement.

The minister quickly apologized for Ray's statement, saying it was unkind and out of place. Since Rev. Don and I were friends, he agreed to consider with me the concepts of our respective faiths in an attempt to detect differences that might indicate why the LDS belief of God is more "physical" than the Methodist belief.

As we proceeded, it seemed we were in agreement with the New Testament account that Jesus was born of virgin birth to

Mary; that He grew up and walked the earth as a man, practiced a building trade and, for about three years, taught His gospel of love and peace.

He atoned for the sins of mankind. He was crucified, died on the cross and was placed in a tomb. We also agreed on the glorious resurrection of the Lord: that His body, which had walked the earth as a man, came up out of the tomb after three days. The resurrected Christ was then eternal, immortal and divine—Godlike qualities only vaguely understood by mortal minds. Though not subject to physical laws as mortals are, still the resurrected Jesus was very real as the Bible relates. The savior invited Thomas to feel the marks of the crucifixion in his hands and side. He prepared breakfast for his apostles. He ate fish and honey with His disciples. He walked and talked with them for forty days.

The question persisted, "Was the resurrected Savior 'physical'?" The answer depends on the meaning given to the word "physical." But since we both accepted the New Testament account of the resurrection, our beliefs seemed about the same at this point. It was on the next point that beliefs seemed to differ.

Methodists believe that God the Father and His Son are <u>one</u> of the "same substance" and essence of the resurrected body of Jesus Christ. LDS believe that God the Father and His Son are <u>two</u> of "like" substance and essence of the resurrected body of Jesus Christ. What is the difference between "the same" and "like" that would prevent the LDS from being Christian? I can find no physical differences at all between "the same" and "like". Reason suggests one concept of God is just as "physical" as the other.

At this point, my minister friend raised his hands and said, "That is a mystery that no one understands, and there is no need to discuss it further." Our discussion ended.

But Rev. Don did not explain Ray's statement, nor answer the question why Ray felt that Latter-day Saints were not Christians. Did Ray have more religious knowledge or better judgment than his minister? Were his unkind comments really caused by Mormon doctrinal beliefs or were they the result of offensive feelings, perhaps caused by Mormons?

A few days later, I went to Ray's home for a friendly chat in the hope that Ray would give me more understanding about his statement. Freely, Ray told me of the hurtful division that had occurred in his family when his close relative had married an active Latter-day Saint and joined the Mormon Church. This had caused bitter feelings and unhappiness in his family. I felt badly, and wished I could have been close enough to him at that time to have perhaps eased the pain and division. It was easy to see why this good man harbored negative feelings toward the Latter-day Saints—which found expression in unkind statements. Offended feelings are the main cause of religious antagonism. When one feels negative about something, almost everything about it seems bad.

CHAPTER 25

Mormons Become Gods?

On a radio talk show over KFYI in Phoenix, I was invited as an LDS church member to be on a panel, along with a Jew, a Catholic, and a 'Born Again Christian' (who was evidently a student of anti-Mormon literature since he had a stack of it with him). But the program was positive, and the 'born again' did not use his negative material. At the conclusion, he followed me to the parking lot where we spent a pleasant hour discussing his unpleasant feelings about Mormonism.

One point he approached this way: "Mr. Andersen, you seem to be a reasonable man. Tell me how in the world you Mormons can possibly believe you may become Gods like your prophet said? 'As man now is, God once was. As God now is, man may become.' That statement is just repulsive to me."

I sympathized with him for his difficulty to fathom how anyone could become like God who we only vaguely comprehend. Then I said, "It is quite easy for LDS to accept this statement. The reason they can is not because they are smarter, or less smart than you are. It is because of their attitude. Since beauty is found in the heart of the beholder, if you really want to understand how Mormons feel, you will need to view LDS teachings about as you view teachings in the Bible. Consider some of these scriptures:

Matt. 5:48 – "Be ye therefore perfect, even as your Father which is in heaven is perfect?" Do you or Christians believe they can be perfect as their Father in Heaven is perfect?

John 10:34-35 – "Jesus answered them, Is it not written in your law, I said, Ye are gods? If he called them gods, unto whom the word of God came, and the scripture cannot be broken." Do you think you are Gods?

John 17:21 – "That they all may be one; as thou, Father, art in me, and I in thee, that they also may be one in us: that the world may believe that thou hast sent me." How do Christians comprehend that?

John 17:22 – "And the glory which thou gavest me I have given them; that they may be one, even as we are one." Our attitude certainly affects comprehension.

John 17:23 – "I in them, and thou in me, that they may be made perfect in one; and that the world may know that thou hast sent me, and hast loved them, as thou hast loved me." How do we comprehend or explain?

Romans 8:16-17 – "the Spirit itself beareth witness with our spirit, that we are the children of God: And if children, then heirs; heirs of God, and joint-heirs with Christ…" Do you or other Christians believe these scriptures will be literally fulfilled in this life or in the future, or are they like "reaching for a star?" Is the Mormon statement about as reasonable and easy to accept as these scriptures are?

Consider the approach of word meanings. As man now is, God once was. As God now is, man may become. Can you or I say exactly what the author meant by his words? Many Christians say God the Father and His son Jesus Christ are one. Since one meaning of the word "God" is "Christ," and one meaning of the word "as" is "like," could the author have said, "Like man now is, Christ once was. Like Christ now is, man may become."

All Christians agree that Christ walked the earth as a man. So: 'Like man now is, Christ once was.' Is there any problem with that?

Can Christians who accept the above scriptures (to be perfect as Father in Heaven is, to be one with the Father and the Son where Christ is, and to become Christ-like in the way we live), then also accept the second part, "Like Christ now is, man may become?"

Those who wish, may feel the Mormon statement is in harmony with scriptures in the New Testament. That is easy to do when one's attitude toward the Mormon statement and the New Testament is the same. The determining factor of what we see in any religion is found in our own attitude. "Seek and ye shall find."

CHAPTER 26

Do Missionaries Steal Sheep?

A local Methodist minister's office door seemed always open to me. The minister had a very alert and perceptive mind. A doctor of divinity, he was honest and direct. To visit with him was a real pleasure for me.

One day as we talked, two missionaries with "The Church of Jesus Christ of Latter-day Saints" on their nametags, walked down the street. The minister's unsmiling eyes followed them until they were not visible.

When his eyes met mine, he smiled and I ventured, "There go two of your best friends. Have you thanked the Lord for them today?"

"Oh, yes," he joked, "I thank the Lord for them all the time they are out stealing my sheep."

With his approval, I tried to soften the irritation I knew he felt, by expressing to him a few concepts.

Recently, members of our family had gone on a tour in Europe. We had been told that England has a "state church" where about 3% of the people attend church on Sunday mornings. In the Scandinavian countries where my grandparents came from, they have a state-supported Lutheran church where attendance is not a lot higher.

Soon after our return to Arizona, an article in our local Mesa paper quoted a recent survey which found that over sixty percent of Mesa residents attend church at least once a month.

"What causes such a tremendous difference in church attendance?" I asked. "Why is the percentage ten to twenty times higher here than over there? Had he considered the reasons for this significant fact?

I suggested that a significant reason for the difference was the impact of missionary efforts in some countries.

"As an example, consider the effect of those two missionaries. What are they going to do all day?"

"Well, steal my sheep," he said.

"What will they say to your sheep?" I asked.

"Testify to them," he responded.

"Correct. The missionaries will try to bear their testimonies that Jesus Christ really lives and loves them; that He has spoken again from heaven for their benefit and blessing; and that He wants them to seek and serve Him. They will encourage those people to read their scriptures, to think deeply on spiritual matters, and to pray to their Heavenly Father for divine direction. After they present their message, they will do their best to get your sheep to ask the Lord if their message is true. Is that correct?"

"Well, yes," he answered.

"Now what percent of those contacted by the missionaries will actually join the Church of Jesus Christ of Latter-day Saints? Actually, it is less than 1%. What will happen to the other 99 percent? Most will be motivated to seek the Lord. They will strengthen their families, buoy up their faith and then attend their own church as stronger, more loyal members. I know from forty years experience that this often happens."

I suggested to my minister friend that LDS missionaries may motivate ten times more of his sheep into activity in their own church than into the LDS Church. I also suggested that perhaps the missionaries motivate even more people into activity into his church than he did.

Would he prefer to have 10 sheep not active in his own church than to risk having one sheep become active in another church? After all, the Holy Spirit does the converting. Do we dare let it have the opportunity?

Months later at a clergy social, I introduced our Arizona Tempe Mission President as "the man who directs the missionaries who are out knocking on your doors. If you ministers have any problem with the missionaries, this is the man to go see." Then I told them the above story about "stealing sheep", emphasizing how missionaries' motivate people into their own churches.

A wonderful Methodist minister friend who was in attendance delightfully commented that in the back of his membership roster was a list of those who attended his church once or twice a year. He said that maybe he should turn that list in to the mission president. He would willingly sacrifice a couple of them to the Mormon Church if the rest would become active.

Another Methodist minister laughed and quipped, "I'm going to tell your Methodist Bishop about you!"

My friend's response was, "Well, maybe the Bishop has a list he'd like to turn in, also!"

Missionary effort, properly performed, brings joy and happiness to the lives of those involved. Our challenge is to carefully practice the Golden Rule so that we benefit and lift each other—not offend. When this happens, missionaries really are good friends to all, and everyone thanks the Lord for them.

❖

CHAPTER 27

Are Mormons Devious Friends?

A delightful Catholic Father who had pastored many years in Mesa, was moving to another parish. He had frequently been in our home, and had supported interfaith understanding. At lunch with him, I asked if he had any parting suggestions for Latter-day Saints. How could they improve relations with their non-Mormon neighbors? He suggested changing our "Welcome Neighbor" program.

"What could possibly by hurtful about that?" I asked. To me, it was an inspired and beautiful program. Nearly in disbelief, I listened as he explained.

"You can understand, Darl, if you will just think. If a family of Catholics from my parish moves into your neighborhood, you go right over and help them move in. Your wife offers to care for the children and she brings a casserole for the evening meal. Later she brings hot bread with homemade jelly. My members like these acts of friendship. Soon they are invited to your church, or invited to read your literature and take your missionary lessons. Being happy with their own church, they refuse your offer, so you stop your friendly gestures, and don't seem interested in being friends anymore. This makes my members conclude that your friendship depends on their interest in your church. Since friendship is something precious, when you use it deviously to get members into your church, it seems dishonest to them, and it makes them mad! Deep!?"

With feelings of pain, I exclaimed, "No, Father Mike! No! The Welcome Neighbor Program is one of the sweetest efforts the LDS church has developed to encourage me, as a typical Mormon, to love my neighbors more and to be of service to them. To tell my neighbors about the LDS Church is, in my opinion, one of the greatest acts of service a Mormon can give. To do that isn't being devious or dishonest one bit.

"Friendship is something that grows naturally. If your members have no interest in something that makes up most of a Mormon's life—namely, his church—then a basis for friendship is quite limited. Whether a friendship develops is determined as much by your member as by the LDS person, and I think you understand that."

He answered, "Yes, I do understand that, but my members do not."

Often, the reaction to our efforts is different than we expect. It helps to know what these reactions are, and why they come. With this understanding, we can be better neighbors and serve more effectively. I learned that our expressions of friendship need to show more sincerity and consistency if we want them to be correctly understood.

Many of our non-Mormon neighbors sincerely feel that every Mormon gesture toward them is devious. They feel that the purpose is to get converts into 'our' church, not really to be friends with them, to be of service to them, or to build faith in Jesus Christ.

Our expressions of love and friendship must be more convincing to them in order to overcome natural denominational barriers. We need more communication as friends to know and do for them what they want for their benefit—not for our personal or selfish desires. The Golden Rule is so effective.

CHAPTER 28

Church of Christ or Cult of Satan?

Curiosity caused me to attend the evening service of a local Protestant church where the announced topic of discussion was "The Mormons." It turned out to be the most painful and miserable meeting of my life. The evident purpose of the meeting was to have a group of 'anti-Mormons' portray my precious LDS faith as being not only false and ridiculous, but cheap and ugly as well. What a horrible experience it was.

The program was convincingly prepared for those with negative feelings toward the LDS, and those without a correct understanding of LDS doctrinal teachings. Even the collection plates were filled with money to abuse Mormonism. Could it be possible that my beautiful religion was repulsive and distasteful as they explained it to be? During sleepless hours that night, their vicious accusations kept returning to my mind, tormenting me, and begging again for specific answers to their main points of attack: false Mormon doctrine, false Mormon prophets, and Mormons not Christians? Sleep finally came after articulating the following reassuring answers to their unkind charges.

During the service, LDS doctrine was twisted to make it appear repulsive. By selecting isolated excerpts from the sayings of various Church leaders to support their charges, these antis painted an ugly picture of LDS doctrine, a picture no knowledgeable Mormon could believe, let alone sacrifice for. For sure they didn't describe my beliefs. A converted Mormon's religion is beautiful and inspiring to him. Anyone who describes it as being ugly does not tell the truth, no matter how words are used. Period.

Much of the doctrine they explained as being "Mormon" I had never heard in a Mormon Church during fifty years of active church participation. In many of their explanations, they had put their own definitions to words used in Mormon statements to make them sound ridiculous. The meanings they attached to these statements completely ignored the great abundance of often-used statements in the LDS scriptures which would have refuted those meanings. I could find no honesty or integrity in any of their positions.

It was a bit amusing to me when they commented that Mormons may deny believing many of the things they presented. "But then," they said, "Mormons really don't know what their own church leaders teach." If Mormons do not know, believe or teach the ugly doctrines described by these antis, then what are they so worked up about? Are they just looking for something to clobber the Mormons with?

Is any person's belief what he says it is, or is it what an antagonist may say it is? Was the Savior's gospel what He said it was, or was it what the Scribes and Pharisees described? Who articulates the doctrines of the Methodists, Catholics, or Lutherans—some antagonist full of hostility and ill-will? The very idea seems so foolish.

The antis severely berated Mormon prophets, especially Joseph Smith and Brigham Young, who were described as having major moral weaknesses. But mostly they were branded as 'false prophets' because they were accused of making predictions that did not happen, and teaching false doctrines. Are Mormon prophets much like the prophets of the Old and New Testaments? Just as human and just as righteous? It appeared that comparing the character, stature and accomplishments of these prophets to those of their accusers (the antis) was about like comparing telephone poles to toothpicks. There is no question who I would rather believe and follow.

What kind of a person is it who assumes to be the all wise judge, and is entitled to attack those millions who may sincerely believe something different than he, when it is evident he does not know the faith and beliefs of those he attacks?

These antis defined Mormonism as, "a non-Christian church, a cult of Satan." Of course, definitions of "a Christian" may be written so as to exclude most anyone desired. But how would the Lord feel if these antis did not keep his commandments any more faithfully than those they accuse of being part of a cult of Satan? Do members of a "cult of Satan" produce as much desirable fruit of the spirit as "true Christians?"

How would the Savior define a Christian? He said, "By their fruits ye shall know them." Rather than just professing to be a Christian with our lips, we should show our faith by our lives. Should a Christian produce the fruits of the spirit rather than the lusts of the flesh as described in Gal. 5:15-26, by living the Golden Rule toward his neighbor, practicing charity as extolled in 1 Cor. 13, and keeping the great commandments to love the Lord and his neighbor as himself? (At least for me the conclusion was clear that the presentation of these faith bashers did not produce the fruits of the spirit which would allow me to conclude that they were more "Christian" than those they condemned.) Certainly their attacks were not the fruits of Christian virtues, nor the Golden Rule.

But near the end of those sleepless hours, a real jolt struck me as some unwanted questions slipped in: Do I love my neighbor as myself? Do I live the golden Rule and practice charity? Does my attitude ever indicate that I feel more intelligent than or superior to my neighbor? Do I thank the Lord for the peace, beauty and inspiration of my neighbors' precious faith, and the many benefits it brings to our neighborhood, schools, community and country? Do I ever express appreciation to him for his faith?

These thoughts were sobering. In considerable sincerity, I plead in prayer to my Father in Heaven to please help me always think and act in harmony with the spirit of His son, Jesus. May my eager efforts to share the beauties of my faith never be felt as being unkind or disrespectful of another's faith. May every person I contact feel I have a real concern and good will for him.

❖

CHAPTER 29

Hypocrisy – The Dreaded Disease of Religious Leaders

Jesus was very forgiving of peoples' sins. This should make us all very happy since He is to be our final judge. In John 8:11, it indicates Jesus did not condemn the woman caught in adultery, but told her to go and sin no more. Also, as He hung on the cross, Jesus prayed to the Father to forgive those who did it, because they knew not what they did. But such forgiveness was not expressed for the sins of the Scribes and Pharisees.

Some of the Scribes and Pharisees received Christ's most severe condemnation. His chastisement of their sins as recorded in Matthew, Chapter 23 is scorching. Their wrongdoing was condemned more by Jesus than was the harlot's, or even those who hung Him on the cross.

It is disturbing that these sinful men were "religious" men. They believed themselves to be the very image of propriety and righteousness. They sat in Moses' seat and professed the faith of their fathers. So what was the nature of their sins that caused the Savior to judge them fools and blind, hypocrites, serpents, children of the adversary and unable to enter the Kingdom?

The Bible tells us of their frequent harassment of Jesus. They were opponents of His gospel of love. They looked for and found fault with his doctrine. They declared it to be heresy and blasphemy, contrary to scripture. They followed Him around to molest his teaching. They fomented and stirred up the people against Him, then accused Him guilty of being the troublemaker. They thought evil in their hearts against Him. Why did they do all these things? As religious leaders, why could they not recognize the light and truth of the Savior's message? Why were they not aware of the error of their attitudes? Why did they not see that they were hypocrites?

Some of the Scribes and Pharisees just loved the plaudits of men. They gloried in their positions of authority. They reveled in the attention and respect shown them. They felt great pride in their offices of leadership. So they developed a hatred for the person and the cause which they saw taking away their valued possessions. They perceived Jesus was taking away their positions of leadership, their place of authority, and their followers.

These sins may not seem any more serious to us than to them. Many justify such human attitudes and reactions among religious leaders today. And who is completely free from such human inclinations? But the all-wise Judge evidently felt their sins were very serious. Can we understand partially why?

1. The hatred in the hearts of these Scribes and Pharisees made them blind to the beauty and truth of the Savior's message. So they were "fools and blind."
2. Their ill will caused them to attack and abuse the Lord. These wrongs they tried to cover up and justify by making accusations against Jesus. So they were "hypocrites."
3. They were antagonists to the Savior's gospel of love, and took the adversary position so they were "Children of the Adversary."

4. With their attitudes and behavior, they were not acceptable in the Kingdom which Jesus proclaimed. So they "would not enter the Kingdom of God."
5. They loved their pride, position and vain glory more than the things of God, justice, mercy and faith. So they "loved self more than God."

Heaven help us so that this most dangerous attitude may not be found among us today. Sometimes there are strong indications of its presence. Those who have the disease may not recognize it. And if they did, they would certainly not admit to it.

"Every way of a man is right in his own eyes, but the Lord searches the hearts." Proverbs 12:2. We don't fool the Lord, just ourselves. Can we honestly search our own hearts, as the Lord would, to avoid fooling ourselves as we use the wisdom of our own eyes. We need some protection against the chance that we could end up with the dreadful disease of those religious leaders the Lord so condemned. It is painful to realize that we are human and as subject to error as they were. The safest method we can find to clearly measure our own behavior as the Lord would measure it is to honestly use the Golden Rule. When we don't do for others what we want them to do for us, we should realize it is a warning signal.

❖

CHAPTER 30

Christ-Centered or Self-Centered?

A Doctor of Divinity had pastored a church and belonged to the Rotary Club in Salt Lake City for several years before he moved to Mesa, Arizona. So our visit was more like brother Rotarians than defensive religious leaders.

This impressive gentleman had worked with Mormon leaders in community projects. He had many good friends among the Latter-day Saints, including President N. Eldon Tanner of the Church's First Presidency. Graciously he spoke of the enviable qualities he had observed among the Mormons, especially their dedication and commitment. He mentioned their strong families, their efforts to care for each other's welfare, their missionary system, their youth activities and their responsiveness to church assignments. He then said he wished his own church members were as committed and as responsive to church assignments of service.

When I asked how he explained the greater dedication and commitment to service to the Lord and their neighbors among Mormons as compared to his own congregation, he hesitated before he answered. "You Mormons have a philosophy of 'work your way to Heaven.' For you, salvation doesn't come from being centered in Christ, and being saved by grace through faith. You believe in earning your salvation by your own works. This makes your works much more apparent and visible."

Since that was a common answer, I referred him to John, 15th chapter, which he quoted to me. There Jesus speaks of himself as the 'true vine,' and to his followers as the branches who should bring forth fruit. Jesus said, "He that abideth in me, and I in him, the same bringeth forth much fruit, for without me ye can do nothing." Surely the most precious, delightful and desirable fruit comes through the 'vine' of Jesus Christ. This most desirable fruit includes such things as charity, love of neighbor, live the Golden Rule, etc. No other vine or philosophy can produce fruit to surpass it.

When the minister agreed with this, I assured him that the deepest commitment to service in my life, as in the lives of other faithful Mormons, springs from a personal testimony of the Lord Jesus Christ. The basic goal in the Church of Jesus Christ of Latter-day Saints is for each member to have a personal testimony of Jesus Christ, to serve Him and to live close to His spirit. So I suggested the enviable fruit that my friend had observed was a result of those individual testimonies and commitment to follow the spirit of the Master.

It seems that to say a particular philosophy can produce more delightful and desirable fruit than through the 'vine' of Jesus Christ would be to deny His superiority. This was not acceptable to either of us.

I suggested that he had lived among the Mormons for many years and knew them to be fairly knowledgeable and mature people, with a deep desire to be of one spirit in service to the Lord. He knew that Mormons were not scurrying around to show 'delightful fruits' just to get stars in their crowns from a less than mature God.

To judge them as being more 'self-centered' than 'Christ-centered' compared to their Christian neighbors, seems foolish. Christians know that being "Christ-centered' brings a more delightful and desirable fruit than being 'self-centered.'

"If ye love me, keep my commandments," the Savior said. To a Mormon Christian, that means trying hard to serve in the spirit of the Master, "even the least of these" and to help build His kingdom. That may be called a "work philosophy."

The desirable fruit seen among Mormon Christians is the result of their personal faith and testimony of Jesus Christ, and the spirit of the Lord that comes to those who know Him. The challenge for LDS is in their belief that the main purpose of the Book of Mormon and living prophets is to increase their love for the Lord and service to their fellow men by living the golden Rule. If this is not evident, then what is their value?

CHAPTER 31

A Burden on My Shoulders

Most members of the Church of Jesus Christ of Latter-day Saints feel their faith gives them many precious blessings. They are humbly grateful for the peace and inspiration they receive, much like every person with a sacred faith. It is hard to see why adversaries describe any inspiring, precious faith as being cheap and repulsive. Thank heaven faith is very personal, not what an opponent may see or explain.

Most every faith has had opponents. Can any opponent be superior in knowledge and understanding, honesty and integrity, love and service just because he may use different words to describe his faith?

The love of the Lord is never found in the spirit and words of contention or abuse. As religious leaders, we usually feel we are servants of the Lord, doing what we should do. But to describe our neighbor's sacred faith without his respect and understanding is not living the great commandment to love our neighbor as ourselves. It is not following the Golden Rule to do for others what we would have them do for us.

Will the Lord judge us guilty of these wrongs? Perhaps the

following experience will add dimension to that question.

Near the village of Palmyra, New York, a Reverend Fred was energetically building up an Assembly of God congregation. Someone had persuaded him to show the anti-Mormon film "The God Makers" at his church. After many weeks of my frequent calling, he finally gave me the time for a short visit.

Respectfully, I expressed love, kindness and appreciation to him for his efforts to build a Christian influence in the community; for the many people he encouraged to have faith in the Lord; and for the high standard of living he taught. Then I mentioned someone had reported that "The God Makers" film had been shown at his church. Though I didn't know what he knew about the truth of the film or the faith of his LDS neighbors, I was there to explain to him that the film was full of distortions and false accusations. Since the LDS religion is beautiful and inspiring to those who believe in it, anyone who describes that religion as being ugly and debasing to believers either doesn't know the truth or simply doesn't tell the truth. This applies to almost everyone's religion as well.

The thrust of this film is an ugly attack against a beautiful faith. It produces many harmful results. It turns neighbor against neighbor. It causes disrespect, ill will and even hatred of others. It causes hurt and abuse. On the other hand, no one is strengthened in the love of the Lord by the film. No one is lifted up and inspired with the Lord's Spirit. No one is encouraged to have more charity, obey the golden Rule, or practice the great commandment to love his neighbor as himself. It is just a hateful exercise to spread false accusations and evil speaking intended to hurt.

Then I suggested that surely the Lord understood this very well, and that some day Reverend Fred would have to account to Him.

We are all so fortunate that the Lord is more charitable and understanding with us than we are with each other. How He will judge Reverend Fred is between him and the Lord. That is not my concern. My concern is that I will also stand to be judged. The Lord may then mention to me the damage and hurt that resulted from the showing of that bad film. My response might be that I was aware of it, and I had been critical of the minister for showing the film while I was on a mission in Palmyra, New York.

The Lord may say that I should have had charity for the minister. Maybe Reverend Fred did not realize the wrong he was doing, the hurt he was causing, or the falseness of the film. So perhaps he should not be condemned when he didn't know he was wrong.

But the Lord may point out that I was the one who knew. Did I go to Reverend Fred in the spirit of love to help him understand this situation so he wouldn't cause such evil? That was a painful thought to me. Could I be partially responsible for the wrong done by the minister because I didn't help him? To me, the thought put a heavy burden on my shoulders. It just made me shudder.

I sincerely thanked Reverend Fred for giving me the opportunity to talk to him and explain the evil of the film. This would take a heavy burden off my shoulders. Now he knew how bad the film was, and could make his decision. I surely didn't want the lord to hold me responsible to any degree for that wrong because I hadn't taken the time and effort to go tell the minister what I knew about it.

CHAPTER 32

The Golden Rule

A few days before we departed for out Senior Couple Mission in Birmingham, Alabama, Pastor Hahn, whose picture is on the front cover of this book, came to our home to bid us farewell. After a short visit, he handed me a letter, and jokingly said as he departed, "Take this letter with you and read it to every Lutheran minister in Alabama."

That letter is astounding to me. It still stirs my emotions.

> RE: Darl Andersen
>
> *Friends, Brothers, Sisters, fellow Lutherans*
>
> *I wish to introduce Darl Andersen.*
> *He is a Mormon.*
> *He is a strong Mormon.*
> *You won't be able to convert him.*
> *HE IS A WONDERFUL PERSON.*
>
> *I have known him for almost 30 years now. We became acquainted when he came to visit me, a newcomer in the city of Mesa, Arizona in 1963.*

We battled, BOY DID WE BATTLE.
I told him every error of Mormonism.
In that terrible strife, Darl and I became dear friends.

I want you to know.
He is sincere in his desire for friendship.
He is sincere in his words of wanting to serve together.
If he calls you "brother" or "sister" he means it.
Darl is willing to forget "doctrine" and be a friend.

If you take the time, eventually you will question, "Is this guy real?" He is. He is a paradox. He is a devout Mormon yet he is sincere in his desire for cooperation. He is not doing and saying the things he does and says to "use" you.

He has a very naive, kind, humble personality - frankly too naive, too kind, too humble to deliberately pull tricks to use you.

He is still a Mormon. I wouldn't deny it. Neither will he, yet, he is a fine person that I believe has done much to help both "Mormons" and "Gentiles" in our community. You will appreciate him as a friend. I respected him so much that he and his wonderful wife were my choice to raise my four children if something happened to my wife and me. He would have raised them Lutheran.

Mesa was a "Mormon" town when I moved there in 1963. There is a temple in Mesa and the economy and politics are largely controlled by the Mormons. I served among them for 27 years in First Ev. Lutheran Church. Because of Darl, I saw many changes in the Mormons, from arrogant people to people who wanted to cooperate and work honorably with main line Protestants and Catholics. I felt a change within myself from wanting to openly destroy them to a willingness to work with them in areas that we could labor. These changes in me came because of my relationship with my friends Darl and Erma.

If you have any questions, CALL ME!
    In His Service
    /s/ Howard C. Hahn Jr.
    Retired Pastor of First Ev. Lutheran Church of Mesa
    Interim Pastor of Lutheran Church of Hope of Phoenix

What caused the amazing change in the heart of Pastor Hahn? The simple practice of the Golden Rule caused the change! But how did that happen?

In his early harsh criticism of Mormonism, Pastor Hahn often mentioned the basic qualities of honesty and integrity. So I began to observe them in him. And when I was able to change *my* attitude to try to do for him, what I wanted him to do for me, the question popped up, "Did *I* show as much honesty and integrity as *he* did?" I didn't know. Did he? The whole direction of our conversation seemed to change from bad to good, from sad to glad.

So when Pastor Hahn recognized sincere honesty among some Mormons he knew, he had integrity great enough to swallow his pride, his hard feelings and opinions as he tried to practice the Golden Rule. That is so evident in his freely given letter to his fellow Lutherans, and everyone else.

Humbly I ponder what I can yet do for him to demonstrate that great love and integrity he continues to show, and help me to honestly live the Golden Rule.

❖